Hurry Up, Harry!

By
Kathleen C. Szaj

Illustrated by
Mark A. Hicks

Paulist Press
New York / Mahwah, N.J.

To Jeffrey and Nicky Young
KCS

To Reece
MAH

Library of Congress Cataloging-in-Publication Data

Szaj, Kathleen C.
    Hurry up, Harry / by Kathleen C. Szaj; illustrated by Mark A. Hicks.
      p.   cm.
    Summary: Harry's dawdling drives his parents crazy, but when they promise not to nag him anymore he does not like the consequences.
    ISBN 0-8091-6653-4
    [1. Punctuality—Fiction. 2. Behavior—Fiction.] I. Hicks, Mark A., ill.
  II. Title.
  PZ7.S9858Hu   1998
  [E]—dc21
                                       98-13310
                                            CIP
                                            AC

Published by Paulist Press
997 Macarthur Boulevard
Mahwah, New Jersey 07430

Printed and bound in Hong Kong

"Harry,
please hurry
up and eat
your breakfast.
You're going
to be late
for school."

That's
my mom
calling me.
She specializes
in wishing that
I'd hurry up at mealtimes.

"Harry, lunch is ready. Please hurry up,
so you can eat your soup while it's still hot."

"Hurry up and finish your dinner, or you
won't get to practice your violin before you have
to leave for your music lesson."

Dad's "Hurry up, Harrys" usually begin
AFTER dinner and at night. He especially likes
to mix in numbers with his hurry-ups.

"Harry, if you
do not hurry up and
find your violin by
the time I count
to **10**, you will
be in serious
trouble."

(Uh-oh . . .
I think I'm
going to need
20 minutes to
find my violin.)

"Harry, I told you **15** minutes ago to take
your bath. You'd better hurry up and get yourself
into that bathroom right away, young man."

(Hey, watch this!
Walking backwards
up the stairs makes
me look like somebody
pressed slow-motion rewind!)

"Harry, isn't 9 o'clock your bedtime? It's 22 minutes past 9 already. Now, you hurry up and get to sleep right this minute."

(Okay,
okay, but
a person
can't *hurry
up* and go
to sleep,
you know.)

My family says so many "Hurry up, Harrys" to me that my little brother, Phillip, thinks that "Hurry-up-Harry" is my real name.

One day, when Grandpa, Phillip and I were taking a shortcut home through the park, we met a lady my grandpa knew. The lady stopped, smiled at us, shook our hands and said, "Very pleased to meet you. What are your names?"

"Hurry-up-Harry!" Phillip shouted, pointing to me.

I put my hand over Phillip's mouth, but it was too late. Phillip tried to bite my finger, I hollered, and Grandpa said that we were going to hurry right home because two boys he knew were not behaving very well.

Last week,
Mom said that
"Dawdle" should
be my middle
name. I said
(very politely),
"Thank you
very much, but
don't you think
'Hurry-up-Harry'
is already
a long
enough
name?"

Dad said I am the most expert
pro-cras-tin-a-tor that he's ever met.
I told Dad that I think it's funny
how long it takes to SAY a
word that describes a
person who takes
a long time
to DO
things.

On Sunday, Grandpa
said, "That boy can
certainly drag his feet!"
So that's what I did . . .
all the way upstairs,
with my feet going
flip-flap-flip-flap,
which was
even BETTER
than walking
backwards in
slow-motion
rewind.
    Grandpa
shook his head
back and forth
and asked my
parents what-
in-heaven's-
name were
they going to
do with me?

That's when
I yelled.

"Everybody
is always
saying,
'Hurry up,
Harry . . .
hurry up,
Harry . . .
hurry up!'
Well, I don't
WANT to
hurry up!
From now on,
I'm going to
take all the time
I want!" I shouted
from the top of
the stairs.

Uh-oh. I knew I was in big trouble now. I ran into
my room, threw myself on my bed and hid my
head under my pillow.

    Dad and Mom followed me into my room.
They sure were quiet. Mom put her hand on
mine and said we had to have a family
conference. In the kitchen. Right away.

While we walked down the stairs to the kitchen, I wished I was taking a ver-r-r-ry long bath . . . or was going straight to bed . . . or even practicing my violin for an extra hour. Instead, I made a horrible face at Phillip, who was sitting in his chair yelling, "Hurry up, Harry. Sit down!" I sat down . . . slo-owly. I was just about ready to say how sorry I was for yelling when Mom said something I could hardly believe.

"Well, Harry, your father and I heard what you said. So, we're not going to say 'Hurry up' anymore. You're old enough now to know when to hurry. You don't need us to tell you all the time."

"So from now on," Dad said, "no more 'Hurry up, Harrys.'"

No more hurrying? This was great! Now I could be as slow as I wanted!

I stayed up extra late that night. No one scolded me to hurry up and go to bed. I watched some TV, made a castle with my building set, fixed myself a cereal snack and read some comic books, until I couldn't keep my eyes open any more at 11 o'clock.

The next morning, when my alarm clock woke me up for school, I was tired and kind of crabby. At least there was no one telling me to hurry and get to school.

Not even when Mom called me for breakfast. I waited for her to tell me to hurry. But she didn't. So, after I told her I'd be right down, I decided to be extra-slow-pokey in getting to my breakfast. First, I got dressed in super slow motion.

Then I invented 4 new ways to tie my shoes.

I combed my hair at least 33 times (I lost count).

When I couldn't
think of one single
other good way to dawdle,
I finally went downstairs for breakfast.

"Yuck!" I said. "My cereal is totally soggy
and tastes like wet cardboard."

"I guess that's because
you took so long
to get ready,"
Mom said.

Just then I heard the school bus horn beeping. That meant the bus had turned the corner onto our street. Now, I'd have to go to school without eating anything. I walked backward all the way upstairs to my room, grabbed my backpack and walked down the stairs, letting only my heels touch the ground. I opened the front door and—

guess what? The bus was nowhere in sight.

"I guess you missed the bus because you took too long getting your backpack," Grandpa said.

"Looks like a nice day for a walk, Harry," Mom said.

Let me tell
you: walking to school
was not much fun. My
hungry stomach growled, and it
felt like my backpack weighed a ton.
But then I thought of a new game: How
many zigzag steps would it take to cross the
sidewalk? Of course, making zigzags takes longer
than walking straight, but at least there was no
one who could say, "Hurry up, Harry."

I got to school 25 minutes late. Miss Driver, my teacher, frowned at me and said I had to stay after school to make up the time I missed. "I can't!" I told her. "I have a baseball game after school!" But, she wouldn't change her mind.

Staying after school sure was boring.
I had to straighten up the books on every shelf,
then line up each desk.

After I finished, I ran all the way to the baseball
field to play with my friends. But when I got
there—you guessed it—everyone had gone home.
I was really upset. I missed my game AND
I had to walk home all by myself.

On the way home, I walked
extra, extra slowly, without
a single zigzag or flip-flap.
I was tired and hungry
and sad.

At dinner, Dad asked me about my day. "It was terrible," I said. "I missed breakfast, missed my bus, was late for school, missed my baseball game and had to walk home all by myself. Taking my time was NOT very much fun. Tomorrow I'm going to hurry up again."

My dad said he was glad to hear me say this. But he wanted me to remember that I didn't have to hurry all the time for everything. "When you're doing things like working on one of your art projects or reading books or playing with Phillip, it's good to take your time," Dad said.

"But when we have places to go and people to see, these people expect us and wait for us," Mom said. "If we dawdle too long, Harry, they don't know where we are or whether we're coming, and they might even be worried about us."

"I get it," I said. "No more missed breakfasts, buses or baseball games for me."

Grandpa smiled, winked at
me and asked me to please pass the
butter. That's when I couldn't help noticing
how much the butter dish I was holding looked like a
submarine. I helped the butter dish sink down to the table
and pushed it slo-owly across, like a sub chugging through
deep water.

"HURRY UP, HARRY!" said Mom, Dad,
Grandpa and Phillip.

And do you know what? I did hurry up.
Because THIS submarine knows how to
"Hurry up, Harry" whenever it has to.
Get it?